D1297963

CAN'T
SCARE ME!

By
**MELISSA
MILICH**

Illustrated By
**TYRONE
GETER**

A Doubleday Book for Young Readers

ACKNOWLEDGMENTS

The author would like to acknowledge Greg Voss for keeping his sense of humor, Karen Wojtyla for having a good ear and a sense of humor, the Sydnor family of Sacramento for taking me in with love and humor, and Nick and Elaine Milich for giving me a happy life and telling me their stories.

A Doubleday Book for Young Readers
Published by
Delacorte Press
Bantam Doubleday Dell Publishing Group, Inc.
1540 Broadway
New York, New York 10036
Doubleday and the portrayal of an anchor with a dolphin are trademarks of
Bantam Doubleday Dell Publishing Group, Inc.
Text copyright © 1995 by Melissa Milich
Illustrations copyright © 1995 by Tyrone Geter

Library of Congress Cataloging in Publication Data
Milich, Melissa.
Can't scare me!/by Melissa Milich; illustrated by Tyrone Geter.
p.   cm.
Summary: Two friends often share a special time in the evening when ghost stories can sometimes be frightening, but a little girl and a special ghost story help Mr. Munroe stop being afraid.
ISBN 0-385-31052-8
[1. Ghosts — Fiction.   2. Fear — Fiction.   3. Afro-Americans — Fiction.]
I. Geter, Tyrone, ill.   II. Title.   III. Title: Can't scare me!
PZ7.M598Mr 1995   [E]— dc20   93-32305 CIP AC

Typography by Lynn Braswell
Manufactured in the United States of America
February 1995
10 9 8 7 6 5 4 3 2 1

*To Ida Mae Sydnor, who inherited her
talent for storytelling from her
father, Mr. Hamond Smith, who told
stories every night as the sky
darkened over his front porch.*

"M<small>R. HAYMAN.</small>"

"Mr. Munroe."

Sometimes that was all they said for *hours.* That and the sound of crickets chirring and rocking chairs rocking and Mama singing in the kitchen. Sometimes an old owl hooting, but always . . .

"Mr. Hayman."

"Mr. Munroe."

Those were the only words until . . . until my papa started telling stories.

Then the rocking of the rocking chairs grew more serious, a steady *mmmhmmm mmmhmmm* almost like a background drum keeping time.

My papa, Mr. Hayman, told wonderful stories,
stories about kings of African tribes, about outlaws
just over the side of the mountain, and about ghosts.
He knew lots of stories about ghosts. Then
Mr. Munroe's rocking chair really speeded up.
Mmmhmmm mmmhmmm mmmhmmm.

   I listened to those stories, me and my sister Ida,
playing with empty milk cartons that we used for
blocks, on the wide front porch of our big house.

"Then the ghost was no more," said my father, ending his story.

Nomore nomore nomore. The rocking chairs always echoed the sound of the words he said. *Nomore nomore.* Just like they were talking.

"You're sure the ghost didn't get him?" said Mr. Munroe.

"I'm sure," said Mr. Hayman.

Sure sure sure sure said the rocking chairs.

But after listening to one of these ghost stories, Mr. Munroe was always afraid to go home. He only lived down the road a piece.

"Mr. Munroe, nothing is going to get you."

"Mr. Hayman, there's ghosts just waitin' to get me."

"Just stay a little longer, Mr. Munroe, and I'll walk you home."

"Okay, Mr. Hayman, as long as you walk me home."

The stories went on. My father hardly stopped long enough to take a sip of lemonade out of a cold glass before he started another story.

The first quarter moon was well toward setting when Mr. Munroe, feeling the chill of the evening breeze, said, "Well, Mr. Hayman, I guess we'd better be gettin' on our way now. The ghosts are gonna be out, will-o'-the-wisps, everything."

"You're a grown man, you can get on home by yourself."

"But Mr. Hayman, you *promised*."

"Then who's gonna walk me home?" my father said. "Sit yourself. I'll tell you another story."

And Mr. Munroe sat back in the wicker rocking chair and forgot about the ghosts out there waiting to get him, because Mr. Hayman was such a marvelous storyteller.

Mr. Munroe came over every night, and the same thing happened. The rocking chair went furiously back and forth, *mmmhmmm mmmhmmm mmmhmmm*, wearing grooves into the porch underneath, and afterward, even though my papa always had nice and calm endings to his stories—so you could go to sleep without nightmares—Mr. Munroe still didn't want to walk himself home.

So one night after they went through it again, I spoke up and said, "I'll walk you home, Mr. Munroe."

I was just a little pipsqueak of a girl, my hair in pigtails all over my head.

And Mr. Munroe said, "Okay, Eugenia."

Mr. Munroe only lived about two hundred yards away. He knew every bush, every rock on his way home. Still, it seemed he jumped as often as a Mexican jumping bean.

"What's that noise?" said Mr. Munroe.

"That's my mama's wind chimes."

"What's that big black shape there?"

"That's the scuppernong bush," I said. "Ain't no more than fifty feet now, Mr. Munroe."

"Ain't you scared of ghosts?" he asked me.

"Shucks. No old white ghost is gonna bother me none."

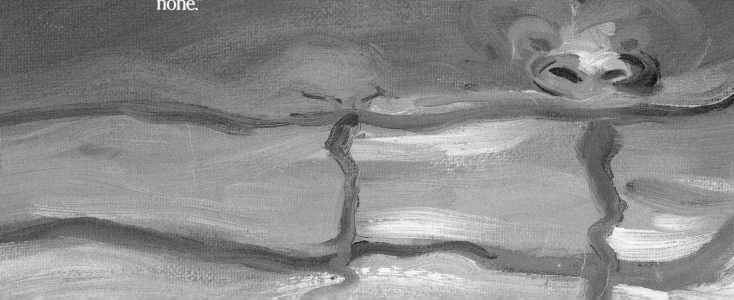

When we got to his house, Mr. Munroe wouldn't let me leave until he turned the kitchen light on. I bet he wished he had a houseful of children like Hayman Fellows did to keep away the bad spirits. Then he locked the door, and then he remembered to say good night. He yelled it through the door. "Good night!"

"Good night, Mr. Munroe."

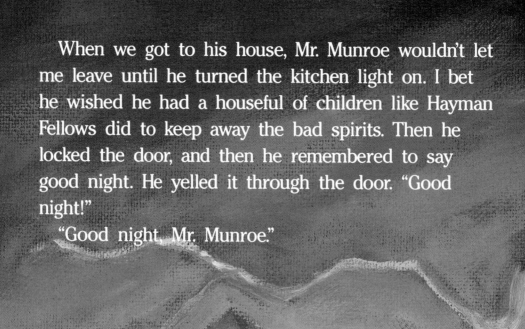

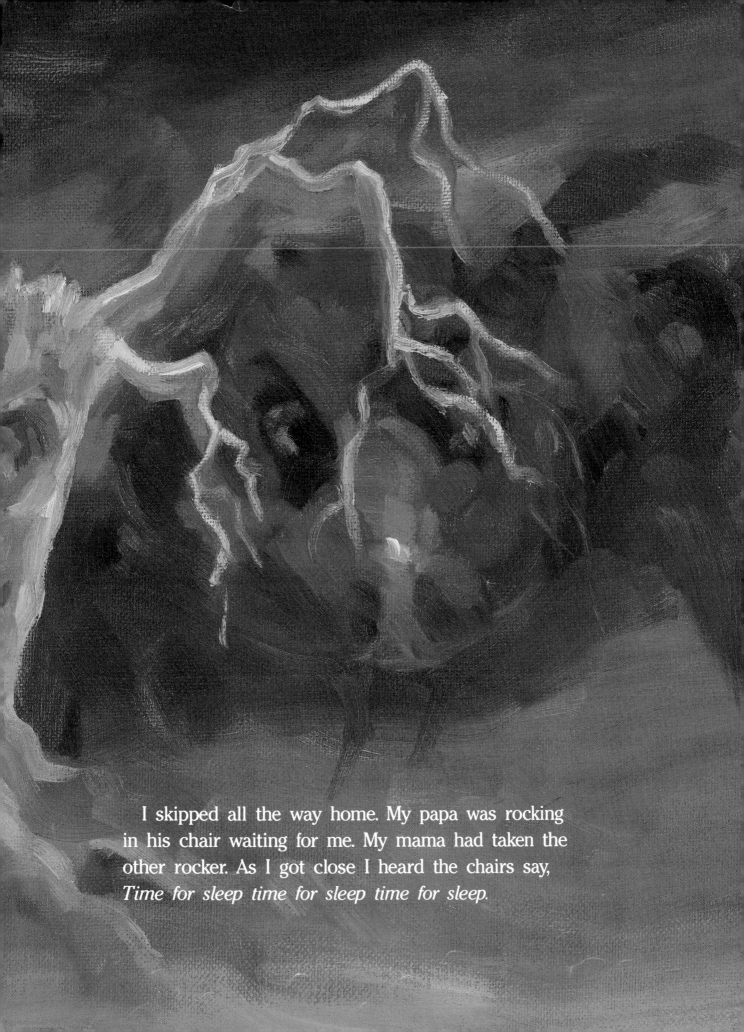

I skipped all the way home. My papa was rocking
in his chair waiting for me. My mama had taken the
other rocker. As I got close I heard the chairs say,
Time for sleep time for sleep time for sleep.

Even though Mr. Munroe hated coming out after dark, my papa's stories seemed more important than ghosts. So Mr. Munroe came every night, and if I didn't walk him home, sometimes he ran the whole way himself, his arms flailing madly, to drive away the ghosts.

One night at supper my father said, "I have to do something about Mr. Munroe."

I didn't know what he was talking about. Then my mother said, "A good God-fearing man does not have to be afraid of ghosts."

So right after supper when Mr. Munroe climbed the
porch steps and sat down in a rocking chair, and my
mama started singing in the kitchen, and Ida and I
were on the porch stacking milk cartons, as the dark
moved in, my father told a story to make Mr. Munroe
not so afraid of ghosts.

"There was once a man by the name of Old Nicholas who used to live in these parts," began my father. He stopped rocking and stared at Mr. Munroe. "Come to think of it, he looked like you."

"Like me?" said Mr. Munroe.

"Yup. Just like you."

Likeyou likeyou likeyou, echoed the rocking chairs.

My father continued, "One night the doctor came riding up to Old Nicholas's house on horseback. He carried a bottle of medicine in his hand.

"The doctor told Old Nicholas, 'This here's a bottle of medicine for the Preacher. He's taken sick to bed. You deliver it to him. I'm going to deliver a baby on the south side of the county.'

"Then the doctor leaned over on his horse and said quite serious, 'If he doesn't get this medicine, there might not be a preacher in church come Sunday.' The doctor said it just like that. Then he rode away. Old Nicholas got his coat and began the walk to the little wooden church where the Preacher lived.

"The night was calm when he started off. He heard a few frogs and crickets and that was all. Then the ghosts woke up. Those ghosts *hate* to hear about people going to church, especially at night. Old Nicholas came to the wooden bridge over the ravine. That bridge is solid in a storm, but on this dark night without a breeze, that bridge swayed and shook worse than a carnival ride. But Old Nicholas kept going.

"Everything came out—apparitions, spirits, every demon for miles around came out of the hills and the swamps that night to try to scare Old Nicholas. Holes opened up deep in the ground. Old Nicholas walked on by. Dead branches turned into poisonous snakes and crossed the road in front of him. Maybe Old Nicholas should've turned back, but he didn't."

"Plum crazy!" interrupted Mr. Munroe.

"No, he was a man on a mission," said my papa. "The Preacher needed that medicine. Those ghosts tried everything, at every turn, at every fork on the trail. At the frog pond a water witch popped out like a jack-in-the-box, the ugliest woman you ever saw, mud in her hair and caked in her long fingernails. But Old Nicholas kept walking. The ghosts called on the weather to bring a storm, a small hurricane to chill his bones. Winds rushed to the mountain, blowing trees sideways, and leaves in whirlpools."

"What'd he do?" interrupted Mr. Munroe.

"Buttoned his coat up tighter, that's all. The only thought crossed his mind was, 'I should have brought me a scarf.'

"Otherwise he stayed on the straight and narrow path."

Narrowpath narrowpath narrowpath, the rocking chairs chorused.

"Old Nicholas had been walking with his head down to keep the dirt from the ghost storm from blowing in his eyes. All of a sudden he realized he was at the church. The ghosts were rising behind him and to his side. Even that ugly old water witch was there dripping swamp juice. Old Nicholas stood up straight and knocked.

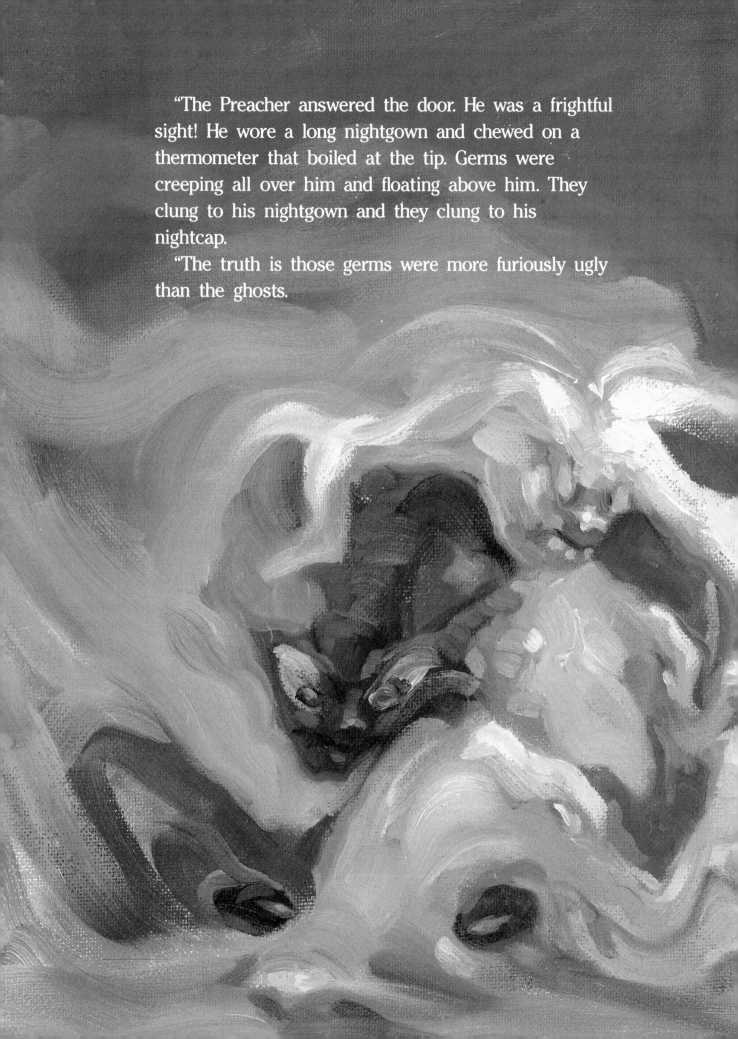

"The Preacher answered the door. He was a frightful sight! He wore a long nightgown and chewed on a thermometer that boiled at the tip. Germs were creeping all over him and floating above him. They clung to his nightgown and they clung to his nightcap.

"The truth is those germs were more furiously ugly than the ghosts.

"The ghosts shrieked. The Preacher shrieked. No one knows who shrieked louder, the ghosts or the Preacher.

"Then . . ." Mr. Hayman paused.

"Then?" asked Mr. Munroe.

Then then then, sang the rocking chairs.

"Then the Preacher sneezed a most loud and powerful sneeze. 'AAAAAAAAAAAAACHOOOOOOOO!'"

"Scared those ghosts clean away. Maybe they were just afraid of catching the flu, but you never saw them again. Old Nicholas gave him the medicine and said, 'See you Sunday in church, Reverend.' Then he turned around and walked home. No ghosts were going to stop him from having a good night's sleep. But the night was calm all over again. The Preacher took his medicine and was well enough to preach in church on Sunday with just an occasional sneeze to interrupt the sermon. And those ghosts haven't been seen in these parts ever since."

Eversince eversince eversince, said the rocking chairs. They slowed down almost to a halt. For a long time the night was still and calm again. Off in the distance we heard a whippoorwill.

"That was a good story," said Mr. Munroe.

"Those ghosts can't scare anyone who isn't afraid of them first," said my father.

"Heck, sometimes adults more afraid than little children," said Mr. Munroe. He yawned big. "Well, I'm ready to get on home. Why don't you walk with me and stretch your legs some?"

"No, I think I'll just sit here a spell."

"Well, maybe I'll just sit here awhile longer too." Mr. Munroe yawned again, his mouth round as a dough-nut. "I'm not even sleepy."

They sat there for a long time, their chairs rocking slowly. *Mmmhmmm mmmhmmm mmmhmmm.* The night paused, seemed to take a deep breath. Then it got dark, darker. The last quarter moon rose at midnight. Mama called from upstairs. She didn't see me hiding in the shadows at the far end of the porch. Mama said, "Hayman! Hayman, come to bed!"

My papa's rocking chair wound down slowly. *Mmmhmmmmm mmmhmmmmm.* Then it stopped dead quiet.

"YOU TOO, EUGENIA!" Mama yelled.

Dang!

"Well, time to go in!" my papa said, and the screen door creaked shut behind him.

"Sleep well," said Mr. Munroe. "I'll see you tomorrow." But my papa was already inside. The last light switched off, and an old owl hooted.

"Well, I guess I BETTER get on HOME myself," said Mr. Munroe, a trifle loudly. He stood on the porch for a long time. He cleared his throat once, twice. Then he started off walking the two hundred yards home.

Dry twigs popped under his boots, loud as the Fourth of July. The scuppernong bush shivered in a sudden wind. Leaves stirred up off the ground like little hurricanes. The frog pond bubbled like poison soup.

He passed the pond, squinting for the water witch. Perhaps he would smell her first. She must smell pretty fierce by now. He sucked a headful of night through his nose, but nope, the night was sweet.

Then he heard something, something like a twig breaking under somebody's feet, somewhere off far behind him.

A cloud floated in front of the moon. The owls
hushed.

There was that sound again . . . a crack of a branch
on the ground . . . feet . . . bare feet running—ghosts
don't wear shoes—ghost feet running after
him . . . fingers reaching out to him . . . a touch on the
arm . . . and—

"Wait for me, Mr. Munroe!"
His eyes were so big I swear I saw my pigtails
reflected in them.

"Oh, it's *you*!" said Mr. Munroe.

"Me," I said. "Eugenia. I came to walk you home. Who was you expecting?"

"Oh, nothin'. Nobody. The only thing I'm gonna expect from now on is good." He looked at me. "I guess you're good?"

"Most of the time."

"Can't ask for more than that."

The clouds moved away from the moon, and the night grew even brighter. There was the scuppernong bush big as a bear. I heard a fish splash in the pond. The wind sent a breeze as old as the world. It made music of the pine needles and the birch trees. The breeze pushed the rocking chairs sitting empty on our front porch, and they didn't seem so lonely anymore.

Mr. Munroe said, "Listen to the night. It is so sweet." We were at his house already. "Good night, child."

"Good night, Mr. Munroe."

The moonlight made sparkles in my path all the way home.